ILLUSTRATED CLASSICS

Snow White

AND OTHER CLASSIC TALES

COMPILED BY

PATRICIA MOORE

MG BOOKS
NEW DELHI (INDIA)

ILLUSTRATED CLASSICS

Snow White

AND OTHER CLASSIC TALES

Published by

An Imprint of

MAANU GRAPHICS

(PUBLISHERS OF GENERAL BOOKS)

5FF, Ganpati Bhawan, 21 Ansari Road,
Darya Ganj, New Delhi-110002
Ph: 65285220, 64138266
E-mail : maanugraphics@yahoo.com
mgbooks.maanu@yahoo.com

Printed at

Satyam Enterprises, Delhi

CONTENTS

A Little Daughter Was Born

SNOW WHITE

Once upon a time, in the middle of winter when the snow-flakes were falling like feathers on the earth, a Queen sat at a window framed in black ebony and sewed. As she sewed and gazed out at the white landscape, she pricked her finger with the needle, and three drops of blood fell on the snow outside, and she thought to herself:

"Oh what wouldn't I give to have a child as white as snow, with cheeks as red as blood, and hair as black as ebony!"

And her wish was granted, for not long after a little daughter was born to her, with skin as white as snow, lips and cheeks as red as blood, and hair as black as ebony. They called her Snow White, and not long after her birth the Queen died.

"Mirror, Mirror, on the Wall

After a year the King married again. His new wife was a beautiful woman, but so proud and overbearing that she couldn't stand any rival to her beauty. She possessed a magic mirror, and when she stood before it gazing at her own reflection and asked:

"Mirror, Mirror, on the wall,
Who's the fairest one of all?"

it always replied:

"You are most fair, my Lady Queen,
None fairer in the land, I ween."

Then she was quite happy, for she knew the mirror always spoke the truth.

But Snow White was growing prettier and prettier every day, and soon she was as beautiful as she could be, and fairer even than the Queen herself.

One day when the Queen asked her mirror the usual question, it replied:

"My Lady Queen, you are fair, 'tis true,
But Snow White is fairer far than you."

Then the Queen flew into the most awful jealous rage, and turned every shade of green. From this hour she hated poor Snow White like poison, and every day her envy, hatred,

Alone in the Big Wood

and malice grew, for envy and jealousy are like evil weeds which spring up and choke the heart. At last she could endure Snow White's presence no longer, and, calling a huntsman to her, she said:

"Take the child out into the wood, and never let me see her face again. You must kill her, and bring me back her lungs and liver, that I may know for certain she is dead."

The huntsman did as he was told and led Snow White out into the wood, but as he was in the act of drawing out his knife to slay her, she began to cry, and said:

"Oh, dear huntsman, spare my life, and I will promise to fly forth into the wild wood and never to return home again."

And because she was so young and pretty the huntsman had pity on her, and said: "Well, run along, poor child." For he thought to himself: "The wild beasts will soon eat her up." And his heart felt lighter because he hadn't had to do the deed himself.

As he turned away a young boar came running past, so he shot it, and brought its lungs and liver home to the Queen as proof that Snow White was really dead. And the

she tried all the others in turn, but one was too long, and another too short, and it was only when she got to the seventh that she found one to suit her exactly. So she lay down upon it, said her prayers like a good child, and fell fast asleep.

When it got quite dark the masters of the little house returned. They were seven dwarfs who worked in the mines, down deep in the heart of the mountain. They lighted their seven little lamps, and as soon as their eyes got accustomed to the glare they saw that someone had been in the room, for all was not in the same order as they had left it.

The first said:

"Who's been sitting on my little chair?"

The second said:

"Who's been eating my little loaf?"

The third said:

"Who's been tasting my porridge?"

The fourth said:

"Who's been eating out of my little plate?"

The fifth said:

wicked woman thought she had made an end of Snow White forever.

Now when poor Snow White found herself alone in the big wood, the very trees around her seemed to assume strange shapes, and she felt so frightened she didn't know what to do. She began to run over the sharp stones, and through the bramble bushes, and the wild beasts ran past her, but they did her no harm. She ran as far as her legs would carry her, and as evening approached she saw a little house, and she stepped inside to rest.

Everything was very small in the little house, but cleaner and neater than anything you can imagine. In the middle of the room there stood a little table covered with a white tablecloth, and seven little plates and forks and spoons and knives and tumblers. Side by side against the wall there were seven little beds, covered with snow-white counterpanes.

Snow White felt so hungry and so thirsty that she ate a bit of bread and a little porridge from each plate, and drank a drop out of each tumbler.

Then feeling tired and sleepy, she lay down on one of the beds, but it wasn't comfortable;

They Were Seven Dwarfs Who Worked the Mines

"Who's been using my little fork?"

The sixth said:

"Who's been cutting with my little knife?"

The seventh said:

"Who's been drinking out of my little tumbler?"

Then the first dwarf looked round and saw a little hollow in his bed, and he asked:

"Who's been lying on my bed?" The others came running round, and cried when they saw their beds:

"Somebody has lain on ours, too."

But when the seventh came to his bed, he started back in amazement, for there he beheld Snow White fast asleep. Then he called the others, who turned their little lamps on the bed, and when they saw Snow White lying there they nearly fell down with surprise.

"Goodness gracious!" they cried, "What a beautiful child!"

And they were so enchanted by her beauty that they did not wake her, but let her sleep on. The seventh dwarf slept with his

Snow White, Fast Asleep

companions one hour in each bed, and in this way he managed to pass the night.

In the morning Snow White awoke, and when she saw the seven little dwarfs she felt very frightened. But they were so friendly and asked her what her name was in such a kind way, that she replied:

"I am Snow White."

"Why did you come to our house?" continued the dwarfs.

Then she told them how her stepmother had wished her put to death, and how the huntsman had spared her life, and how she had run the whole day till she had come to their little house. The dwarfs, when they had heard her sad story, asked her:

"Will you stay and keep house for us, cook, make the beds, do the washing, sew and knit? And if you give satisfaction and keep everything neat and clean, you shall want for nothing."

"Yes," answered Snow White, "I will gladly do all you ask." And so she took up her abode with them. Every morning the dwarfs went into the mountain to dig for

destroy her, for as long as she felt she had a rival her jealous heart left her no rest. At last she hit upon a plan.

She stained her face and dressed herself up as an old peddler wife, so that she was quite unrecognizable. In this guise she went over the hills till she came to the house of the seven dwarfs. There she knocked at the door, calling out at the same time:

"Fine wares to sell, fine wares to sell!"

Snow White peeped out of the window, and called out:

"Good day, mother, what have you to sell?"

"Good wares, fine wares," she answered; "laces of every shade and description," and she held one up that was made of some gay colored silk.

"Surely I can let the honest woman in," thought Snow White; so she unbarred the door and bought the pretty lace.

"Good gracious, child," said the old woman. "Come, I'll lace you up properly for once."

gold, and in the evening, when they returned home, Snow White always had their supper ready for them. But during the day the girl was left quite alone, so the good dwarfs warned her, saying:

"Beware of your stepmother. She will soon find out you are here, and whatever you do, don't let anyone into the house."

Now the Queen never dreamed but that she was once more the most beautiful woman in the world; so stepping before her mirror one day she said:

"Mirror, mirror, on the wall,

Who's the fairest one of all?" and the mirror replied:

"My Lady Queen, you are fair, 'tis true, But Snow White is fairer far than you. Snow White, who dwells with the seven little men, Is twice as fair as you again." When the Queen heard these words she was nearly struck dumb with horror, for the mirror always spoke the truth, and she knew now that the huntsman must have deceived her, and that Snow White was still alive.

She pondered day and night how she might

"Beware of Your Stepmother"

Snow White, suspecting no evil, stood before her and let her lace up her bodice, but the old woman laced her so quickly and so tightly that it took Snow White's breath away, and she fell down as if dead.

"Now you are no longer the fairest," said the very wicked woman, and she hastened away.

In the evening the seven dwarfs came home, and you may think what a fright they got when they saw their dear Snow White lying on the floor, as still and motionless as a dead person. They lifted her up tenderly, and when they saw how tightly laced she was they cut the lace in two, and she began to breathe a little and gradually came back to life.

When the dwarfs heard what had happened, they said: "Depend upon it, the peddler wife was none other than the bad Queen. In future you must be sure to let no one in, if we are not at home."

As soon as the wicked old Queen got home she went straight to her mirror, and said:

"Mirror, mirror, on the wall,

Who's the fairest one of all?" and the mirror answered as before:

"My Lady Queen, you are fair, 'tis true, But Snow White is fairer far than you. Snow White, who dwells with the seven little men, Is twice as fair as you again."

When she heard this she became as pale as death, because she saw at once that Snow White must be alive again.

"This time," she said to herself, "I will think of something that will make an end of her once and for all."

And by the witchcraft which she understood so well she made a poisonous comb; then she dressed herself up and assumed the form of another old woman. So she went over the hills till she reached the house of the seven dwarfs, and knocking at the door she called out:

"Fine wares for sale."

Snow White looked out of the window and said:

"You must go away, for I may not let anyone in."

"But surely you are not forbidden to look out?" said the old woman, and she held up the poisonous comb for her to see.

It pleased the girl so much that she let herself be taken in, and opened the door. When they had settled their bargain, the old woman said:

"Now I'll comb your hair properly for you, for once and for all."

Snow White thought no evil, but hardly had the comb touched her hair than the poison worked and she fell down unconscious.

"Now, my fine lady, you're really done for this time," said the wicked woman, and she made her way home as fast as she could.

Fortunately it was now near evening, and the seven dwarfs returned home. When they saw Snow White lying dead on the ground, they at once suspected that her wicked stepmother had been at work again; so they searched till they found the poisonous comb, and the moment they pulled it out of her head Snow White came to herself again, and told them what had happened. Then they warned her once more to be on her guard, and to open the door to no one.

Dressed Up as an Old Peddler

As soon as the Queen got home she went straight to her mirror, and asked:

"Mirror, mirror, on the wall,

Who's the fairest one of all?"

and it replied as before:

"My Lady Queen, you are fair, 'tis true,

But Snow White is fairer far than you.

Snow White, who dwells with the seven little men,

Is twice as fair as you again."

When she heard these words she trembled and shook with rage.

"Snow White shall die," she cried; "yes, though it cost me my own life."

Then she went to a little secret chamber, which no one knew of but herself, and there she made a poisonous apple. Outwardly it looked beautiful, with red skin, so that everyone who saw it longed to eat it, but anyone who might do so would certainly die on the spot. When the apple was quite finished she stained her face and dressed herself up

Still and Motionless

as a peasant, and so she went over the hills to the seven dwarfs'. She knocked at the door, as usual, but Snow White put her head out of the window and called out:

"I may not let anyone in; the seven dwarfs have forbidden me to do so."

"Are you afraid of being poisoned?" asked the old woman. "See, I will cut this apple in half. I'll eat from one side and you can eat the other."

But the apple was so cunningly made that only one half was poisonous. Snow White longed to eat the tempting fruit, and when she saw that the peasant woman was eating it herself, she couldn't resist the temptation any longer, and stretching out her hand she took the poisonous half.

But hardly had the first bite passed her lips than she fell down dead on the ground. Then the eyes of the cruel Queen sparkled with glee, and laughing aloud she cried:

"As white as snow, as red as blood, and as black as ebony, this time the dwarfs won't be able to bring you back to life."

The Poisonous Comb

When she got home she asked the mirror:

"Mirror, mirror, on the wall,
Who's the fairest one of all?"

and this time it replied:

"You are most fair, my Lady Queen,
None fairer in the land, I ween."

Then her jealous heart was at rest — at least, as much at rest as a jealous heart can ever be.

When the little dwarfs came home in the evening they found Snow White lying on the ground, and she neither breathed nor stirred. They lifted her up, and looked round everywhere to see if they could find anything poisonous about. They unlaced her bodice, combed her hair, washed her with water and wine, but all in vain; she was dead and remained dead.

They placed her on a bier, and all the seven dwarfs sat round it, weeping and sobbing for three whole days. At last they made up their minds to bury her, but she looked as blooming as a living being, and her cheeks were still such a lovely color, that they said:

Outwardly, It Looked Beautiful

"We can't hide her away in the cold ground."

So they had a coffin made of clear glass, and they laid her in it, and wrote on the lid in golden letters that she was a royal Princess. Then they put the coffin on the top of the mountain, and one of the dwarfs always remained beside it and kept watch over it.

And the very birds of the air came and bewailed Snow White's death, first an owl, and then a raven, and last of all a little dove.

Snow White lay a long time in the coffin, and she always looked the same, just as if she were fast asleep, and she remained as white as snow, as red as blood, and her hair as black as ebony.

Now it happened one day that a Prince came to the wood and passed by the dwarfs' house. He saw the coffin on the hill, with the beautiful Snow White inside it, and when he had read what was written on it in golden letters, he said to the dwarf:

"Give me the coffin. I'll give you whatever you like for it."

Only One Half was Poisonous

But the dwarf said: "No, we wouldn't part with it for all the gold in the world."

"Well, then," he replied, "give it to me, because I can't live without Snow White. I will cherish and love it as my dearest possession."

He spoke so sadly that the good dwarfs had pity on him, and gave him the coffin, and the Prince made his servants bear it away on their shoulders. Now it happened that as they were going down the hill they stumbled over a bush, and jolted the coffin so violently that the poisonous bit of apple Snow White had swallowed fell out of her throat. She gradually opened her eyes, lifted up the lid of the coffin, and sat up alive and well.

"Oh! Dear me, where am I?" she cried.

The Prince answered joyfully, "You are with me," and he told her all that had happened, adding, "I love you better than anyone in the whole wide world. Will you come with me to my father's palace and be my wife?"

Snow White consented, and went with him, and the marriage was celebrated with great pomp and splendor.

A Coffin of Glass

Now Snow White's wicked stepmother was one of the guests invited to the wedding feast. When she had dressed herself very gorgeously for the occasion, she went to the mirror, and said:

"Mirror, mirror, on the wall,

Who's the fairest one of all?"

and the mirror answered:

"My Lady Queen, you are fair, 'tis true,

But Snow White is fairer far than you."

Snow White and her Prince lived happily ever after.

The Old Shoemaker

THE ELVES AND THE SHOEMAKER

There was once a shoemaker, who, through no fault of his own, became so poor that at last he had nothing left but just enough leather to make one pair of shoes.

He cut out the shoes at night, so as to set to work upon them next morning; and as he had a good conscience, he laid himself quietly down in his bed and fell asleep.

In the morning, after he had said his prayers, and was going to get to work, he found the pair of shoes made and finished, and standing on his table.

He was very much astonished, and could not tell what to think, and he took the shoes in his hand to examine them more clearly;

they were so well made that every stitch was in its right place, just as if they had come from the hand of a master-workman.

Soon after, a purchaser entered, and as the shoes fitted him very well, he gave more than the usual price for them, so that the shoemaker had enough money to buy leather for two more pairs *of* shoes.

He cut them out at night, and intended to set to work the next morning with fresh spirit; but that was not to be, for when he got up they were already finished, and a customer even gave him so much money that he was able to buy leather enough for four new pairs.

Early next morning he found the four pairs also finished, and so it always happened; whatever he cut out in the evening was worked up by the morning, so that he was soon making a good living, and in the end became very well to do.

One night, not long before Christmas, when the shoemaker had finished cutting out, and before he went to bed, he said to his wife,

"How would it be if we were to sit up tonight and see who it is that does us this service?"

His wife agreed, and set a light to burn. Then they both hid in a corner of the room, behind some coats that were hanging up, and they began to watch.

As soon as it was midnight they saw come in two neatly formed little men, who seated themselves before the shoemaker's table, and took up the work that was already prepared, and began to stitch, to pierce, and to hammer so cleverly and quickly with their little fingers that the shoemaker's eyes could scarcely follow them, so full of wonder was he.

And they never left off until everything was finished and was standing ready on the table, and then they jumped up and ran off.

The next morning the shoemaker's wife said to her husband, "Those little men have made us rich, and we ought to show ourselves grateful. With all their running about, and having little to cover them, they must be very cold.

"Spruce and Dandy Boys Are We!"

'll tell you what: I will make little shirts, coats, waistcoats, and breeches for them, and knit each of them a pair of stockings, and you shall make each of them a pair of shoes."

The husband consented willingly, and at night, when everything was finished, they laid the gifts together on the table, instead of the cut-out works, and placed themselves so that they could observe how the little men would behave.

When midnight came, they rushed in, ready to set to work, but when they found, instead of the pieces of prepared leather, the neat little garments ready for them, they stood a moment in surprise, and then they showed the greatest delight.

With great swiftness they took up the pretty garments and slipped them on, singing:

"What spruce and dandy boys are we! No longer cobblers we will be."

Then they hopped and danced about, jumping over the chairs and tables, and at last they danced out the door.

Whatever he Took in Hand Prospered

From that time they were never seen again; but it always went well with the shoemaker as long as he lived, and whatever he took in hand prospered.

Martin, Michael, and Jack

THE THREE TREASURES OF THE GIANTS

Long, long ago, there lived an old man and his wife who had three sons; the eldest was called Martin, the second Michael, while the third was named Jack. One evening they were all seated round the table, eating their supper of bread and milk.

"Martin," said the old man suddenly, "I feel that I cannot live much longer. You, as the eldest, will inherit this hut, but, if you value my blessing, be good to your mother and brothers."

"Certainly, father; how can you suppose I should do them wrong?" replied Martin indignantly, helping himself to all the best bits in the dish as he spoke. The old man saw nothing, but Michael looked on in surprise,

One Fine Morning All Three Set Out

and Jack was so astonished that he quite forgot to eat his own supper.

A little while after, the father fell ill, and sent for his sons, who were out hunting, to bid him farewell. After giving good advice to the two eldest, he turned to Jack.

"My boy," he said, "you have not got quite as much sense as other people, but if Heaven has deprived you of some of your wits, it has given you a kind heart. Always listen to what it says, and take heed to the words of your mother and brothers, as well as you are able!" So saying the old man sank back on his pillows and died.

The crics of grief uttered by Martin and Michael sounded through the house, but Jack remained by the bedside of his father, still and silent, as if he were dead also. At length he got up, and going into the garden, hid himself in some trees, and wept like a child, while his two brothers made ready for the funeral.

No sooner was the old man buried than Martin and Michael agreed that they would go into the world together to seek their fortunes, while Jack stayed at home with their

"You are a Nice Pair!"

mother. Jack would have liked nothing better than to sit and dream, by the fire, but the mother, who was very old herself, declared that there was no work for him to do, and that he must seek it with his brothers.

So, one fine morning, all three set out; Martin and Michael carried two great bags full of food, but Jack carried nothing. This made his brothers very angry, for the day was hot and the bags were heavy, and about noon they sat down under a tree and began to eat.

Jack was as hungry as they were, but he knew that it was no use asking for anything; and he threw himself under another tree, and wept bitterly.

"Another time perhaps you won't be so lazy, and will bring food for yourself," said Martin, but to his surprise Jack answered:

"You are a nice pair! You talk of seeking your fortunes so as not to be a burden on our mother, and you begin by carrying off all the food she has in the house!"

This reply was so unexpected that for some moments neither of the brothers made any

The Door of the Castle Stood Open

answer. Then they offered their brother some of their food, and when he had finished eating they went their way once more.

Towards evening they reached a small hut, and knocking at the door, asked if they might spend the night there. The man, who was a wood-cutter, invited them in, and begged them to sit down to supper.

Martin thanked him, but being very proud, explained that it was only shelter they wanted, as they had plenty of food with them; he and Michael at once opened their bags and began to eat, while Jack hid himself in a corner.

The wife, on seeing this, took pity on him, and called him to come and share their supper, which he gladly did, and very good he found it. At this, Martin regretted deeply that he had been so foolish as to refuse, for his bits of bread and cheese seemed very hard when he smelt the savory soup his brother was enjoying.

"He shan't have such a chance again," thought he; and the next morning he insisted on plunging into a thick forest where they were likely to meet nobody.

This Room was a Mass of Gold

For a long time they wandered hither and thither, for they had no path to guide them; but at last they came upon a wide clearing, in the midst of which stood a castle. Jack shouted with delight, but Martin, who was in a bad temper, said sharply:

"We must have taken a wrong turn! Let us go back."

"Idiot!" replied Michael, who was hungry, too, and like many people when they are hungry, very cross also. "We set out to travel through the world, and what does it matter if we go to the right or to the left?" And, without another word, he took the path to the castle, closely followed by Jack, and after a moment by Martin likewise.

The door of the castle stood open, and they entered a great hall, and looked about them. Not a creature was to be seen, and suddenly Martin – he did not know why – felt a little frightened.

He would have left the castle at once, but stopped when Jack boldly walked up to a door in the wall and opened it. He could not for very shame be outdone by his younger brother, and passed behind him into another

He Made Up His Mind

splendid hall, which was filled from floor to ceiling with great pieces of copper money.

The sight quite dazzled Martin and Michael, who emptied all the provisions that remained out of their bags, and heaped them up instead with handfuls of copper.

Scarcely had they done this when Jack threw open another door, and this time it led to a hall filled with silver. In an instant his brothers had turned their bags upside down, so that the copper money tumbled out on to the floor, and were shovelling in hand-fuls of the silver instead.

They had hardly finished, when Jack opened yet a third door, and all three fell back in amazement, for this room was a mass of gold, so bright that their eyes grew sore as they looked at it. However, they soon recovered from their surprise, and quickly emptied their bags of the silver, and filled them with gold instead. When they would hold no more, Martin said:

"We had better hurry off now lest somebody else should come, and we might not know what to do;" and, followed by Michael, he hastily left the castle. Jack lingered behind for a few minutes to put pieces of gold, silver, and copper into his pocket, and to eat the food that his brothers had thrown down in the first room.

Then he went after them, and found them lying down to rest in the midst of a forest. It was near sunset, and Martin began to feel hungry, so, when Jack arrived, he bade him return to the castle and bring the bread and cheese that they had left there.

"It is hardly worth doing that," answered Jack; "for I picked up the pieces and ate them myself."

At this reply both brothers were beside themselves with anger, and fell upon the boy, beating him, and calling him names, till they were quite tired.

"Go where you like," cried Martin with a final kick; "but never come near us again." And poor Jack ran weeping into the woods.

The next morning his brothers went home, and bought a beautiful house, where they lived with their mother like great lords.

Jack remained for some hours in hiding, thankful to be safe from his tormentors; but when no one came to trouble him, and his back did not ache so much, he began to think what he had better do. At length he made up his mind to go to the castle and take away as much money with him as would enable him to live in comfort for the rest of his life.

This being decided, he sprang up, and set out along the path which led to the castle. As before, the door stood open, and he went on till he had reached the hall of gold, and there he took off his jacket and tied the sleeves together so that it might make a kind of bag.

He then began to pour in the gold by handfuls, when, all at once, a noise like thunder shook the castle. This was followed by a voice, hoarse as that of a bull, which cried:

"I smell the smell of a man." And two giants entered.

"So, little worm! It is *you,* who steal our treasures!" exclaimed the biggest. "Well, we have got you now, and we will cook you for supper!" But here the other giant drew him aside, and for a moment or two they whispered together. At length the first giant spoke:

"The Dinner of an Emperor!"

"To please my friend I will spare your life on condition that, for the future, you shall guard our treasures. If you are hungry take this little table and rap on it, saying as you do so: 'The dinner of an Emperor!' and you will get as much food as you want."

With a light heart Jack promised all that was asked of him, and for some days enjoyed himself mightily. He had everything he could wish for, and did nothing from morning till night; but by-and-by he began to get very tired of it all.

"Let the giants guard their treasures themselves," he said to himself at last; "I am going away. But I will leave all the gold and silver behind me, and will take nought but you, my good little table."

So, tucking the table under his arm, he started off for the forest, but he did not linger there long, and soon found himself in the fields on the other side. There he saw an old man, who begged Jack to give him something to eat.

"You could not have asked a better person," answered Jack cheerfully. And signing to him

"Two Hundred Hussars, Forward!"

to sit down with him under a tree, he set the table in front of them, and struck it three times, crying:

"The dinner of an Emperor!" He had hardly uttered the words when fish and meat of all kinds appeared on it!

"That is a clever trick of yours," said the old man, when he had eaten as much as he wanted. "Give it to me in exchange for a treasure I have which is still better. Do you see this cornet? Well, you have only to tell it that you wish for an army, and you will have as many soldiers as you require."

Now, since he had been left to himself, Jack had grown ambitious, so, after a moment's hesitation, he took the cornet and gave the table in exchange.

The old man bade him farewell, and set off down one path, while Jack chose another, and for a long time he was quite pleased with his new possession.

Then, as he felt hungry, he wished for his table back again, as no house was in sight, and he wanted some supper badly. All at once he remembered his cornet, and a wicked thought entered his mind.

"My Bag Will Give You Many Castles"

"Two hundred hussars, forward!" cried he. And the neighing of horses and the clanking of swords were heard close at hand. The officer who rode at their head approached Jack, and politely inquired what he wished them to do.

"A mile or two along that road," answered Jack, "you will find an old man carrying a table. Take the table from him and bring it to me."

The officer saluted and went back to his men, who started at a gallop to do Jack's bidding.

In ten minutes they had returned, bearing the table with them.

"That is all, thank you," said Jack; and the soldiers disappeared inside the cornet.

Oh, what a good supper Jack had that night, quite forgetting that he owed it to a mean trick. The next day he breakfasted early, and then walked on towards the nearest town. On the way thither he met another old man, who begged for something to eat.

"Certainly, you shall have something to

eat," replied Jack. And, placing the table on the ground, he cried:

"The dinner of an Emperor!" and all sorts of good dishes appeared. At first the old man ate greedily, and said nothing; but, after his hunger was satisfied, he turned to Jack and said:

"That is a very clever trick of yours. Give the table to me, and you shall have something still better."

"I don't believe that there's anything better," answered Jack.

"Yes, there is. Here is my bag; it will give you as many castles as you can possibly want."

Jack thought for a moment; then he replied: "Very well, I will exchange with you." And passing the table to the old man, he hung the bag over his arm.

Five minutes later he summoned five hundred lancers out of the cornet and bade them go after the old man and fetch back the table.

Now that by his cunning he had obtained possession of the three magic objects, he resolved to return to his native place. Smearing his face with dirt, and tearing his clothes so as to look like a beggar, he stopped the passersby and, on pretense of seeking money or food, he questioned them about the village gossip.

In this manner he learned that his brothers had become great men, much respected in all the country round. When he heard that, he lost no time in going to the door of their fine house and imploring them to give him food and shelter; but the only thing he got was hard words, and a command to beg elsewhere.

At length, however, at their mother's entreaty, he was told that he might pass the night in the stable. Here he waited until everybody in the house was sound asleep, when he drew his bag from under his cloak, and desired that a castle might appear in that place; and the cornet gave him soldiers to guard the castle, while the table furnished him with a good supper.

In the morning, he caused it all to vanish, and when his brothers entered the stable they found him lying on the straw.

Passing the Night in the Stable

Jack remained here for many days, doing nothing, and – as far as anybody knew – eating nothing. This conduct puzzled his brothers greatly, and they put such constant questions to him, that at length he told them the secret of the table, and even gave a dinner to them, which far outdid any they had ever seen or heard of.

But though they had solemnly promised to reveal nothing, somehow or other the tale leaked out, and before long reached the ears of the King himself. That very evening his chamberlain arrived at Jack's dwelling, with a request from the King that he might borrow the table for three days.

"Very well," answered Jack, "you can take it back with you. But tell his majesty that if he does not return it at the end of the three days I will make war upon him."

So the chamberlain carried away the table and took it straight to the King, telling him at the same time of Jack's threat, at which they both laughed till their sides ached.

Now the King was so delighted with the table, and the dinners it gave him, that when

The Chamberlain to Stay and Dine

the three days were over he could not make up his mind to part with it.

Instead, he sent for his carpenter, and bade him copy it exactly, and when it was done he told his chamberlain to return it to Jack with his best thanks.

It happened to be dinner time, and Jack invited the chamberlain, who knew nothing of the trick, to stay and dine with him.

The good man, who had eaten several excellent meals provided by the table in the last three days, accepted the invitation with pleasure, even though he was to dine in a stable, and sat down on the straw beside Jack.

"The dinner of an Emperor!" cried Jack. But not even a morsel of cheese made its appearance.

"The dinner of an Emperor!" shouted Jack in a voice of thunder. Then the truth dawned on him; and, crushing the table between his hands, he turned to the chamberlain, who, bewildered and half-frightened, was wondering how to get away.

"Tell your false King that tomorrow I will

The King Saw It Was Useless

destroy his castle as easily as I have broken this table."

The chamberlain hastened back to the palace, and gave the King Jack's message, at which he laughed more than before, and called all his courtiers to hear the story. But they were not quite so merry when they woke next morning and beheld ten thousand horsemen, and as many archers, surrounding the palace.

The King saw it was useless to hold out, and he took the white flag of truce in one hand, and the real table in the other, and set out to look for Jack.

"I committed a crime," said he; "but I will do my best to make up for it. Here is your table, which I own with shame that I tried to steal, and you shall have besides my daughter as your wife!"

There was no need to delay the marriage when the table was able to furnish the most splendid banquet that ever was seen, and after everyone had eaten and drunk as much as they wanted, Jack took his bag and commanded a castle filled with all sorts of

Not a Week Passed Without a Visit

treasures to arise in the park for himself and his bride.

At this proof of his power the King's heart died within him.

"Your magic is greater than mine," he said; "and you are young and strong, while I am old and tired. Take, therefore, the sceptre from my hand, and my crown from my head, and rule my people better than I have done."

So at last Jack's ambition was satisfied. He could not hope to be more than a King, and as long as he had his cornet to provide him with soldiers he was secure against his enemies.

He never forgave his brothers for the way they had treated him, though he presented his mother with a beautiful castle, and everything she could possibly wish for.

In the center of his own palace was a treasure chamber, and in this chamber the table, the cornet, and the bag were kept as the most prized of all his possessions, and not a week passed without a visit from him to make sure they were safe. He reigned long and well, and died a very old man, beloved by his people.

But his good example was not followed by his sons and his grandsons. They grew so proud that they were ashamed to think that the founder of their line had once been a poor boy; and as they and all the world could not fail to remember it, as long as the table, the cornet, and the bag were shown in the treasure chamber, one King, more foolish than the rest, thrust them into a dark and damp cellar.

For some time the kingdom remained, though it became weaker and weaker every year that passed. Then, one day, a rumor reached the King that a large army was marching against him.

Vaguely he recollected some tales he had heard about a magic cornet which could provide as many soldiers as would serve to conquer the earth, and which had been removed by his grandfather to a cellar.

Thither he hastened that he might renew his power once more, and in that black and slimy spot he found the treasures indeed.

But the table fell to pieces as he touched it, in the cornet there remained only a few fragments of leathern belts which the rats had gnawed, and in the bag nothing but broken bits of stone.

And the King bowed his head to the doom that awaited him, and in his heart cursed the ruin wrought by the pride and foolishness of himself and his forefathers.

Always Smashing, Upsetting, Breaking!

HOW MOTI WON THE WAR

Once upon a time there was a youth called Moti, who was very big and strong, but the clumsiest creature you can imagine. So clumsy was he that he was always putting his great feet into the bowls of sweet milk which his mother set out on the floor to cool, always smashing, upsetting, breaking, until at last his father said to him:

"Here, Moti, are fifty silver pieces which are the savings of years; take them and go and make your living or your fortune if you can."

Then Moti started off early one spring morning with his thick staff over his shoulder, singing gaily to himself as he walked along.

In one way and another he got along very well until a hot evening when he came to a

His Money Had Been Stolen!

certain city where he entered the travelers' serai, or inn, to pass the night. Now a serai is generally just a large square enclosed by a high wall with an open colonnade along the inside all round to accommodate both men and beasts, and with perhaps a few rooms in towers at the corners for those who are too rich or too proud to sleep by their own camels and horses.

Moti, of course, was a country lad and had lived with cattle all his life, and he wasn't rich and he wasn't proud, so he just borrowed a bed from the innkeeper, set it down beside an old buffalo who reminded him of home, and in five minutes was fast asleep.

In the middle of the night he woke, feeling that he had been disturbed, and putting his hand under his pillow found to his horror that his bag of money had been stolen!

He jumped up quietly and began to prowl around to see whether anyone seemed to be awake, but, though he managed to arouse a few men and beasts by falling over them, he walked in the shadow of the archways round the whole serai without coming across a likely thief.

"It is Our House!"

He was just about to give up when he overheard two men whispering, and one laughed softly, and, peering behind a pillar, he saw two Afghan horsedealers counting out his bag of money! Then Moti went back to bed.

In the morning Moti followed the two dealers outside the city to the horsemarket in which their horses were offered for sale. Choosing the best-looking horse amongst them he went up to it and said:

"Is this horse for sale? May I try it?" and, the merchants assenting, he scrambled up on its back, dug in his heels, and off they flew. Now Moti had never been on a horse in his life, and had so much to do to hold on with both hands as well as with both legs that the animal went just where it liked, and very soon broke into a break-neck gallop and made straight back to the serai where it had spent the last few nights.

"This will do very well," thought Moti as they whirled in at the entrance. As soon as the horse had arrived at its stable it stopped of its own accord and Moti immediately rolled off; but he jumped up at once, tied the beast up, and called for some breakfast. Presently the dealers appeared, out of breath and furious, and claimed the horse.

"What do you mean?" cried Moti, with his mouth full of rice. "It's my horse; I paid you fifty pieces of silver for it – quite a bargain, I'm sure!"

"Nonsense! It is *our* horse," answered one of the Afghans, beginning to untie the bridle.

"Leave off," shouted Moti, seizing his staff; "if you don't let my horse alone I'll crack your skulls! You thieves! I know you! Last night you took my money, so today I took your horse; that's fair enough!"

Now they began to look a little uncomfortable, but Moti seemed so determined to keep the horse that they resolved to appeal to the law, so they went off and laid a complaint before the King that Moti had stolen one of their horses and would not give it up nor pay for it.

Presently a soldier came to summon Moti to the King; and, when he arrived and made his obeisance, the King began to question him as to why he had galloped off with the horse in this fashion. But Moti declared that he had got the animal in exchange for fifty pieces of silver, whilst the horse merchants vowed that the money they had on them was what they had received for the sale of other horses.

In one way and another the dispute got so confusing that the King (who really thought that Moti had stolen the horse) said at last: "Well, I tell you what I will do. I will lock something into this box before me, and if he guesses what it is, the horse is his, and if he doesn't, then it is yours."

To this Moti agreed, and the King arose and went out alone by a little door at the back of the court, and presently came back clasping something closely wrapped up in a cloth under his robe, slipped it into the little box, locked the box, and set it up where all might see.

"Now," said the King to Moti, "guess!"

It happened that when the King had opened the door behind him, Moti noticed that there was a garden outside: without waiting for the King's return he began to think what could be got out of the garden small enough to be shut in the box.

"Now," said the King, "Guess!"

"Is it likely to be a fruit or a flower? No, not a flower this time, for he clasped it too tight. Then it must be a fruit or a stone. Yet not a stone, because he wouldn't wrap a dirty stone in his nice clean cloth.

"Then it is a fruit! And a fruit without much scent, or else he would be afraid that I might smell it. Now what fruit without much scent is in season just now?

"When I know that I shall have guessed the riddle!"

Moti was a country lad, and used to work in his father's garden. He knew all the common fruits, so he thought he ought to be able to guess right; but not to let it seem too easy, he gazed up at the ceiling with a puzzled expression, looked at the floor with an air of wisdom, his fingers pressed against his forehead, and then he said, slowly, with his eyes on the king:

"It is freshly plucked! It is round and it is red! It is a pomegranate!"

Now the King knew nothing about fruits except that they were good to eat; and, as for seasons, he asked for whatever fruit he

"It is a Pomegranate!"

wanted whenever he wanted it, and saw that he got it; so to him Moti's guess was like a miracle, and clear proof not only of his wisdom but of his innocence, for it *was* a pomegranate that he had put into the box!

Of course when the King marveled and praised Moti's wisdom, everybody else did so, too; and, whilst the horsetraders went off crestfallen, Moti took the horse and entered the King's service.

Very soon after this, Moti, who continued to live in the serai, came back one wet and stormy evening to find that his precious horse had strayed. Nothing remained of him but a broken halter cord, and no one knew what had become of him. After inquiring of everyone who was likely to know, Moti seized the cord and his big staff and sallied out to look for him.

Away and away he tramped out of the city and into the neighboring forest, tracking hoof-marks in the mud.

Presently it grew late, but still Moti wandered on until suddenly in the gathering darkness he came right upon a tiger who was contentedly eating his horse.

"You Thief!"

"You thief!" shrieked Moti, and ran up, and, just as the tiger, in astonishment, dropped a bone – *whack* came Mori's staff on his head with such good will that the beast was half-stunned and could hardly breathe or see. Then Moti continued to shower upon him blows and abuse until the poor tiger could hardly stand, whereupon Moti tied the broken halter round his neck and dragged him back to the serai.

"If you had my horse," he said, "I will at least have you, that's fair enough!" And he tied him up securely by the head and heels, much as he used to tie the horse; then, the night being far gone, he flung himself beside him and slept soundly.

You cannot imagine anything like the fright of the people in the serai, when they woke up and found a tiger – very battered but still a tiger – securely tethered amongst themselves and their beasts!

Men gathered in groups talking and exclaiming, and finding fault with the innkeeper for allowing such a dangerous beast into the serai, and all the while the innkeeper was just as troubled as the rest, and

The Monarch Himself Came Down

none dared go near the place where the tiger stood blinking miserably on everyone, and where Moti lay stretched out snoring like thunder.

At last news reached the King that Moti had exchanged his horse for a live tiger; and the monarch himself came down, half disbelieving the tale, to see if it were really true. Someone at last awaked Moti with the news that his royal master was come; and he arose yawning, and was soon delightedly explaining and showing off his new possession.

The King, however, did not share his pleasure at all, but called up a soldier to shoot the tiger, much to the relief of all the inmates of the serai except Moti.

If the King,, however, was before convinced that Moti was one of the wisest of men, he was now still more convinced that he was the bravest, and he increased his pay a hundredfold, so that our hero thought that he was the *luckiest* of men.

A week or two after this incident the King sent for Moti, who on arrival found his master in despair. A neighboring monarch, he explained, who had many more soldiers than he, had declared war against him, and he was at his wits' end, for he had neither money enough to buy him off nor soldiers enough to fight him – what was he to do?

"If that is all, don't you trouble," said Moti. "Turn out your men, and I'll go with them, and we'll soon bring this robber to reason."

The King began to revive at these hopeful words, and took Moti off to his stable where he bade him choose for himself any horse he liked. There were plenty of fine horses in the stalls, but to the King's astonishment Moti chose a poor little rat of a pony that was used to carry grass and water for the rest of the stable.

"But why do you choose that beast?" said the King.

"Well, you see, your majesty," replied Moti, "there are so many chances that I may fall off, and if I choose one of your fine big horses I shall have so far to fall that I shall probably break my leg or my arm, if not my neck, but if I fall off this little beast I can't hurt myself much."

A very comical sight was Moti when he rode out to the war. The only weapon he carried was his staff, and to help him to keep his balance on horseback he had tied to each of his ankles a big stone that nearly touched the ground as he sat astride the little pony.

The rest of the King's cavalry were not very numerous, but they pranced along in armor on fine horses. Behind them came a great rabble of men on foot armed with all sorts of weapons, and last of all was the King with his attendants, very nervous and ill at ease. So the army started.

They had not very far to go, but Moti's little pony, weighted with a heavy man and two big rocks, soon began to lag behind the cavalry, and would have lagged behind the infantry too, only they were not very anxious to be too early in the fight, and hung back so as to give Moti plenty of time.

Moti jogged along more and more slowly for some time, until at last, getting impatient at the slowness of the pony, he gave him such a tremendous thwack with his staff that the pony completely lost his temper and bolted. First one stone became untied and rolled

A Poor Little Rat of a Pony

away in a cloud of dust to one side of the road, whilst Moti nearly rolled off, too, but he clasped his steed valiantly by its ragged mane, and, dropping his staff, held on for dear life.

Then fortunately the other rock broke away from his other leg and rolled thunderously down a neighboring ravine. Meanwhile the advanced cavalry had barely time to draw to one side when Moti came dashing by, yelling bloodthirsty threats to his pony: "You wait till I get hold of you! I'll skin you alive! I'll wring your neck! I'll break every bone in your body!"

The cavalry thought that this dreadful language was meant for the enemy, and were filled with admiration for his courage. Many of their horses were quite upset by this whirlwind that galloped howling through their midst, and in a few minutes, after a little plunging and rearing and kicking, the whole troop were following on Moti's heels.

Far in advance, Moti continued his wild career. Presently he came to a great field of castor-oil plants, ten or twelve feet high, big and bushy, but quite green and soft. Hoping

The Pony Bolted

to escape from the back of his fiery steed, Moti grasped one in passing, but its roots gave way, and he dashed on, with the whole plant looking like a young tree flourishing in his grip!

The enemy was in battle array, advancing over the plain, their King with them confident and cheerful, when suddenly from the front came a desperate rider at a furious gallop.

"Sire!" he cried, "Save yourself! The enemy is coming!"

"What *do* you mean?" said the King.

"Oh, sire!" panted the messenger, "Fly at once, there is no time to lose. Foremost of the enemy rides a mad giant at a furious gallop. He flourishes a tree for a club and is wild with anger, for as he goes he cries: 'You wait till I get hold of you! I'll skin you alive! I'll wring your neck! I'll break every bone in your body!' Others ride behind, and you will do well to retire before this whirlwind of destruction comes upon you!"

Just then out of a cloud of dust in the distance, the King saw Moti approaching at a hard gallop, looking indeed like a giant

"Sire! Save Yourself!"

compared with the little beast he rode, whirling his castor-oil plant, which in the distance might have seemed an oak tree, and the sound of his revilings and shoutings came down upon the breeze!

Behind him the dust cloud moved to the sound of the thunder of hoofs, whilst here and there flashed the glitter of steel. The sight and the sound struck terror into the King, and, turning his horse, he fled at top speed, thinking that a regiment of yelling giants was upon him; and all his force followed him as fast as they might go.

One fat officer alone could not keep up on foot with that mad rush, and as Moti came galloping up he flung himself on the ground in abject fear. This was too much for Moti's excited pony, who shied so suddenly that Moti went flying over his head like a sky rocket, and alighted right on the top of his fat foe.

Quickly regaining his feet, Moti began to swing his plant round his head and to shout:

"Where are your men? Bring them up and I'll kill them. My regiments! Come on, the whole lot of you! Where's your King? Bring

Moti the Wise

him to me. Here are all my fine fellows coming up and we'll each pull up a tree by the roots and lay you all flat and your houses and towns and everything else! Come on!"

But the poor fat officer could do nothing but squat on his knees with his hands together, gasping. At last, when he got his breath, Moti sent him off to bring his King, and to tell him that if he was reasonable his life should be spared.

Off the poor man went, and by the time the troops of Moti's side had come up and arranged themselves to look as formidable as possible, he returned with his King. The latter was very humble and apologetic, and promised never to make war any more, to pay a large sum of money, and altogether do whatever his conqueror wished.

So the armies on both sides went rejoicing home, and this was really the making of the fortune of clumsy Moti, who lived long and contrived always to be looked up to as a fountain of wisdom, valor, and discretion by all except his own relatives, who could never understand what he had done to be considered so much wiser than anyone else!

"Ho, Jack! Where Are You Going?"

JACK AND THE BEANSTALK

Once upon a time a boy named Jack lived with his mother on their farm. They were very poor. Although they worked very hard, the dry, rocky soil gave up barely enough to feed them and their last remaining cow, Bossy.

Although it grieved Jack's mother to do it, she decided at last that the cow must be sold. One day, she called to Jack. "There is a fair two towns away," she said, "and you Jack must go and get the best price you can for Bossy. It is impossible for us to feed her any longer, but if you go and get a good price, we should be able to live on that for at least a little while."

So off Jack went, sad to be losing so good and faithful an animal as Bossy had been, but at the same time glad enough to have a little adventure.

He hadn't gone far when suddenly a funny little man stepped out onto the road. "Ho, Jack!" the man called to him. "Where are you going with that fine looking animal?"

Jack was surprised. He wondered how this stranger knew his name, and why he was so complimentary about Bossy, who had certainly seen better days.

"I'm off to the fair to sell my cow," Jack replied.

"Well, perhaps I can save you some steps and bother," said the little stranger. "Seeing as how I'm somewhat in the market for a cow myself."

What good luck, Jack thought. His mother would be very pleased if he managed to sell Bossy and return home so quickly. "What will you give me for her?" he asked.

"Five beans," said the stranger. "Do you know how many make five?"

"Yes," said Jack proudly. "Three in my mouth and one in each hand, that's five. But I don't know as five is enough for such a fine cow as Bossy."

"But these aren't just any five beans," the stranger said, lowering his voice and looking about as if to see if anyone else could hear him. "These are magic beans."

"Magic?" asked Jack. "What's magic about them?"

The stranger winked. "Take them home and you'll find out soon enough," he promised.

Jack wasn't quite sure. His mother wouldn't think that five beans were so much, but if they were really magic, there could be an end to all of their problems. He thought and thought, and at last made up his mind. "I'll take them!" he said to the stranger. He patted Bossy on the top of her head and handed her rope to the stranger.

He put the beans in his pocket, turned on his heels, and headed home.

"What! So soon!" his mother said. "You must have gotten a very good price very quickly for you to be back from the fair so soon."

"These Are Magic Beans"

"I didn't even have to go all the way," said Jack proudly. "I sold Bossy, and look what I got!" He held out his hand with the five beans.

"What! You sold the whole cow for five beans!" His mother couldn't believe her ears. "That's not even enough to make supper for us!"

"But these are magic beans," Jack said. He hated when his mother was angry or disappointed with him.

"Magic! Fine! This is what I think of your magic!" And his mother grabbed the beans and threw them out of the window. She ran from the room crying, and both of them went to bed without dinner that night.

When Jack woke up in the morning, his little room was shadowed and dark. He rubbed his eyes, wondering why the bright sun that shone each morning hadn't wakened him. He went to the window and looked out. But all he could see was green, green, green, blocking out everything even up to the sky.

Jack ran outside to see what it could be.

There, towering over the house and

"This Is What I Think of Magic!"

the farm, was a beanstalk, but a beanstalk bigger than the usual kind as a king's palace was from the tiny farmhouse that Jack and his mother lived in. Stalk and leaf, branch and shoot, it reached higher into the sky than Jack could see.

"Look, Mother!" Jack said excitedly. "I told you that the beans were magic!"

"I still don't see the good of it," his mother replied. "What will it do for us to have a beanstalk that throws shadows over everything else?"

"I'm going to climb it!" Jack said. "I'm going to see what's on the very, very top!"

And climb he did. But the longer he climbed, the taller the beanstalk seemed to be. At last, quite exhausted, he reached the top.

Jack looked around. In both directions stretched a wide road. At one end, far away as it was, he could see a palace that seemed to float amidst the clouds that surrounded it.

Seeing that there was nothing in the opposite direction, Jack set off toward the palace. He walked and walked. It seemed to

"I'm Going to Climb It!"

him as though the distance to the palace was even greater than that from the ground to the top of the beanstalk. But on and on he went, until he could make out the moat, the doors, and the windows of the tallest towers. At last he stood in front of the rough wooden bridge that stretched across the moat to the double doors of the palace entrance.

Everything was as still as still could be. There was no sign of life to be seen nor heard. There was nothing to do, Jack thought, but to go straight in.

He squared his shoulders, straightened his spine, and walked quickly across the bridge.

Jack could barely reach the great round rings that hung upon the doors. But grasping one as hard as he could, he pushed with all his might until the door swung open and he was inside.

Jack tiptoed cautiously along the stone corridor, peering into the enormous rooms that lined each side.

As he made his way deeper inside the palace, he heard an enormous rumbling sound coming from deep inside. Hugging the

He Pushed with All His Might

wall, he tiptoed along to see where it was coming from. As he got closer to the sound, it seemed to him as if the whole palace was shaking.

He peeked into an enormous chamber. There, on the biggest chair Jack had ever seen, sat snoring the biggest giant he could ever have imagined. The great rumbling noise was the snoring of the giant as he slept.

Jack had to hold himself very stiff to keep his knees from shaking with fright. The giant's knees were about as high as the top of Jack's head reached, and all around the red booted legs of the sleeping giant were sacks full of glittering gold coins. Some lay about on the floor, and some glittered on top of the sacks that they were crammed into. It seemed to Jack as though the giant must have been counting his wealth and fallen asleep in the midst of the enormous inventory.

If he and his mother had only a tiny portion of the giant's wealth, it seemed to Jack they'd never have to worry about anything ever again. The thought gave him a kind of courage, and slowly, quietly, and very, very carefully he crept closer to the sleeping giant, until he was close enough to grab one of the money sacks by the ties around its neck, and shoving it inside his shirt, make his way out again as carefully as he had come in.

Jack hurried down the corridor to the palace entrance, shivering with fear as he ran every time an especially loud snore from the giant shook the palace to its very foundations.

His heart racing as fast as his legs, his legs racing as fast as his feet could carry them, at last Jack found himself on the bridge that spanned the moat and back on the road again. Even here he didn't slacken, but ran as fast as he could to where the road gave way to the top of the beanstalk.

Shifting the heavy bag of coins from side to side as he scurried down, Jack finally fell in a scramble at the bottom of the beanstalk.

He could scarcely believe he was back in his own farmyard again, so strange and bewildering had been all of the sights at the top of the beanstalk.

But now he collected himself and went looking for his mother, to show her their new found treasure.

Jack's mother could scarcely believe the story of the palace and the giant, but when Jack emptied the bag of gold coins in front of her, she laughed and cried and declared he was the best son in the whole world. Straight away, she apologized for ever having doubted Jack and his magic beans. Now, she declared, they could live happily ever after.

"But no," said Jack. "This one bag is just the beginning of the treasures in the giant's palace. I must go back for more."

Try as she would to dissuade him, Jack was insistent. Not for one mere bag of gold had he braved the fearsome giant. There was more treasure to be had, and he was the boy to have it.

The very next morning Jack made his way back up the beanstalk. When he got to the top everything was as it had been, and he made his way quickly to the giant's palace.

Stealing inside, he passed the room where the giant was once again asleep. Ignoring the rumbling thunder of his snoring, Jack tiptoed into an enormous room that he realized was the giant's kitchen.

A Kind of Courage

Enormous pots, pans, and kettles of all shapes hung about on the walls. But Jack took no interest in these. He started to walk out, to look for more treasure-laden chambers, when he spotted a plump white goose sitting on a table. Afraid that she might start honking and so awaken the giant, Jack snatched her up and tucked her under his arm.

But no sooner had he moved the goose, than she let fall a shiny egg.

Still clutching her tightly, Jack stooped down to retrieve it. Amazingly, it hadn't broken on the hard stone floor. Jack soon realized why.

The egg was of solid gold, as bright and shiny as the coins he had gotten the previous day, but far larger.

He immediately realized the worth of this estimable bird, and headed for the beanstalk and home, knowing that this goose was the equal of any other treasure he might find.

You can imagine Jack's mother's surprise when he produced the goose and its golden outlay. Although his mother had lived on a farm all of her life, she had never seen the like.

Jack Snatched Her Up

"This bird will be our fortune, Jack!" she exclaimed. "Now we will have surely everything we need."

"Not quite yet, mother," said Jack. "For I mean to try the beanstalk yet one more time."

Nothing his mother could say would change Jack's mind, so determined was he to steal into the giant's palace once again. Thus it was that early the next morning he again made his way up the beanstalk and into the giant's castle.

Jack did not know what he might find, only he knew it would be something wondrous. Thus, when once inside the palace, he heard not the rumble of the giant's snoring, but a sweet sound drifting from above his head, he was not surprised.

Looking up, he saw a beautiful golden harp. That its shape was of a woman did not surprise him; that the harp could play such wonderful music without anyone putting hands to its strings, did.

Jack had no idea what such a harp might be worth, but he knew he had to have it. He jumped up to pluck it down from the wall on

"This Bird Will Be Our Fortune!"

which it rested. He put it under his arm and started to steal out of the palace.

But as soon as he started running, a movement like wind swept through the harp, and of its own accord it began to wail: "Oh master, oh master, Oh lackaday

Come faster, come faster, For I'm stolen away!"

Jack ran as fast as he could, but the golden harp never ceased its wailing. The faster he ran, the louder the song became.

At last it was loud enough to rouse the sleeping giant.

The whole palace shook as Jack heard the heavy footsteps behind him.

The footsteps became faster and louder, the golden harp wailed higher and faster, and Jack's heart beat fastest of all as he raced toward the top of the beanstalk.

At last he was there. Clutching the golden harp to him, he sprang from branch to branch, making his way ever downward.

At last he reached the ground. "Mother,

"For I'm Stolen Away!"

Mother!" he shouted. "Come quickly, and bring the old ax from the barn!"

His mother came running out. Jack took the ax from her and started hacking away at the bottom of the beanstalk.

He could feel it shake and rumble, but he knew it was not from his own efforts; it was the giant, coming closer and closer. Any moment, he would be climbing down the beanstalk itself.

Jack redoubled his efforts. He chopped harder and harder.

The giant was climbing down now, his feet looking like great boulders as he placed them on lower and lower branches of the beanstalk.

Jack heaved and swung with all of his might.

The giant's bulk was blotting out the sun, and a great shadow lay over the little farm and all of the surrounding fields. The giant came closer.

With the mightiest effort he had ever made in his life, Jack swung the ax again at the very roots of the beanstalk. The weight of the giant

Crashing Down Completely

weakened the stalk still further, and it began to sway and waver.

Suddenly, it came crashing down completely, carrying the giant with it and burying him beneath the weight of its leafy green branches.

"Oh master, oh master!" wailed the harp.

But the giant was no more.

"Oh master, oh master!" wailed the harp in a softer voice, as she turned toward Jack. "You are my master now!" she sang out.

And so saying, the harp and the goose and Jack and his mother lived in great happiness and riches forever after.

He Sewed for Dear Life

THE BRAVE LITTLE TAILOR

One summer's day a little tailor sat on his table by the window in the best of spirits and sewed for dear life. As he was sitting thus a peasant woman came down the street, calling out: "Good jam to sell! Good jam to sell!"

This sounded sweetly in the tailor's ears. He put his frail little head out of the window and shouted: "Up here, my good woman, and you'll find a willing customer."

The woman climbed up the three flights of stairs with her heavy basket to the tailor's room, and he made her spread out all the pots in a row before him. He examined them all, lifted them up and smelled them, and said at last: "This jam seems good. Weigh me four

"Who Invited You?"

ounces of it, my good woman; and even if it's a quarter of a pound I won't stick at it."

The woman, who had hoped to make a good sale, gave him what he wanted, but went away grumbling wrathfully.

"Now Heaven shall bless this jam for my use," cried the little tailor, "and it shall sustain and strengthen me." He fetched some bread out of a cupboard, cut a round off the loaf, and spread the jam on it. "That won't taste amiss," he said; "but I'll finish that waistcoat first before I take a bite."

He placed the bread beside him, went on sewing, and out of the lightness of his heart kept on making his stitches bigger and bigger. In the meantime the smell of the sweet jam rose to the ceiling, where heaps of flies were sitting, and attracted them to such an extent that they swarmed on to it in masses.

"Ha! Who invited you?" asked the tailor, and chased the unwelcome guests away. But the flies, who didn't understand, refused to be warned off", and returned again in even greater numbers.

At last the little tailor, losing all patience,

reached out to his chimney corner for a duster, and exclaiming, "Wait, and I'll give it to you," he beat them mercilessly with it. When he left off he counted the slain, and no fewer than seven lay dead before him with outstretched legs.

"What a brave fellow I am!" said he, and was filled with admiration at his own courage. "The whole town must know about this." And in great haste the little tailor cut out a wide belt, hemmed it, and embroidered on it in big letters, "Seven at one blow."

"What did I say, the town? No, the whole world shall hear of it," he said; and his heart beat for joy as a lamb wags its tail.

The tailor strapped the belt round his waist and set out into the wide world, for he considered his workroom too small a field for his prowess. Before he set forth he looked round about him, to see if there was anything in the house he could take with him on his journey; but he found nothing except an old cheese, which he took.

In front of the house he observed a bird that had been caught in some bushes, and this he put into his pack beside the cheese. Then he went on his way merrily, and being light and agile he never felt tired.

His way led up a hill, on the top of which sat a powerful giant, who was calmly surveying the landscape.

The little tailor went up to him, and greeting him cheerfully said: "Good day, friend, here you sit at your ease viewing the whole wide world. I'm just on my way there. What do you say to accompanying me?"

The giant looked contemptuously at the tailor and said: "What a poor wretched little creature you are!"

"That's a good joke," answered the little tailor, and unbuttoning his coat he showed the giant the belt. "There now, you can read what sort of a fellow I am."

The giant read, "Seven at one blow," and thinking they were human beings the tailor had slain, he conceived a certain respect for the little man. But first he thought he'd test him, so taking up a stone in his hand he squeezed it till some drops of water ran out. "Now you do the same," said the giant, "if you really wish to be thought strong."

"Seven At One Blow"

"Is that all?" said the little tailor, "That's child's play to me."

So he dived into his pack, brought out the cheese, and pressed it till the whey ran out. "My squeeze was in sooth better than yours," said he.

The giant didn't know what to say, for he couldn't have believed it of the little fellow. To prove him again, the giant lifted a stone and threw it so high that the eye could hardly follow it. "Now, my little pygmy, let me see you do that."

"Well thrown," said the tailor; "but, after all, your stone fell to the ground. I'll throw one that won't come down at all." He dived into his pack again, and grasping the bird in his hand, he threw it up into the air. The bird, enchanted to be free, soared up into the sky and flew away never to return.

"Well, what do you think of that little piece of business, friend?" asked the tailor.

"You can certainly throw," said the giant; "but now let's see if you can carry a proper weight." With these words he led the tailor to a huge oak tree which had been felled to

"Let Me See You Do That"

the ground and said: "If you are strong enough, help me to carry the tree out of the wood."

"Most certainly," said the little tailor. "Just you take the trunk on your shoulder. I'll bear the top and branches, which is certainly the heaviest part." The giant laid the trunk on his shoulder, but the tailor sat at his ease among the branches; and the giant, who couldn't see what was going on behind him, had to carry the whole tree and the little tailor in the bargain. There he sat behind in the best of spirits, lustily whistling a tune, as if carrying the tree were mere sport.

The giant, after dragging the heavy weight for some time, could get on no further and shouted out: "Hi! I must let the tree fall."

The tailor sprang nimbly down, seized the tree with both hands as if he had carried it the whole way, and said to the giant: "Fancy a big lout like you not being able to carry a tree!"

They continued to go on their way together, and as they passed by a cherry tree the giant grasped the top of it, where the ripest fruit hung, gave the branches into the

The Tailor Sprang Nimbly Down

tailor's hand, and bade him eat. But the little tailor was far too weak to hold the tree down, and when the giant let go, the tree swung back into the air, bearing the little tailor with it.

When he had fallen to the ground again without hurting himself, the giant said: "What! Do you mean to tell me you haven't the strength to hold down a feeble twig?"

"It wasn't strength that was wanting," replied the tailor. "Do you think that would have been anything for a man who has killed seven at one blow? I jumped over the tree because the huntsmen are shooting among the branches near us. Do the like if you dare."

The giant made an attempt, but couldn't get over the tree, and stuck fast in the branches, so that here too the little tailor had the better of him.

"Well, you're a fine fellow, after all," said the giant. "Come and spend the night with us in our cave." The little tailor willingly consented to do this, and following his friend they went on till they reached a cave where several other giants were sitting round a fire, each holding a roast sheep, of which he was eating.

More Room to Turn Around In

The little tailor looked about him and thought: "Yes, there's certainly more room to turn round in here than in my workshop," The giant showed him a bed and bade him lie down and have a good sleep. But the bed was too big for the little tailor, so he didn't get into it, but crept away into the corner.

At midnight, when the giant thought the little tailor was fast asleep, he rose up, and taking his big iron walking-stick, he broke the bed in two with a blow, and thought he had made an end of the little tailor.

At early dawn, the giants went off to the wood and quite forgot about the little tailor, till all of a sudden they met him trudging along in the most cheerful manner. The giants were terrified at the apparition, and, fearful lest he should slay them, they all took to their heels as fast as they could.

The little tailor continued to follow his nose, and after he had wandered about for a long time he came to the courtyard of a royal palace, and feeling tired he lay down on the grass and fell asleep.

While he lay there the people came, and

"Quite Ready to Enter the King's Service"

looking him all over read on his belt: "Seven at one blow."

"Oh!" they said, "what can this great hero of a hundred fights want in our peaceful land? He must indeed be a mighty man of valor." They went and told the King about him, and said what a weighty and useful man he'd be in time of war, and that it would be well to secure him at any price.

This counsel pleased the King, and he sent one of his courtiers down to the little tailor, to offer him, when he awoke, a commission in their army. The messenger remained standing by the sleeper and waited till he stretched his limbs and opened his eyes, when the messenger tendered his proposal.

"That's the very thing I came here for," the tailor answered. "I am quite ready to enter the King's service." So he was received with all honor and given a special house of his own to live in.

But the other officers resented the success of the little tailor, and wished him a thousand miles away. "What's to come of it all?" they asked each other. "If we quarrel with him

About to Make Him an Offer

he'll let out at us, and at every blow seven will fall. There'll soon be an end of us."

So they resolved to go in a body to the King and to all send in their papers of resignation. "We are not made," they said, "to hold out against a man who kills seven at one blow."

The King was grieved at the thought of losing all his faithful servants for the sake of one man, and he wished heartily that he had never set eyes on the tailor, or that he could get rid of him. But the King didn't dare to send him away, for he feared he might kill him along with his people, and place himself on the throne. He pondered long and deeply over the matter and finally came to a conclusion.

He sent to the tailor and told him that, seeing what a great and warlike hero he was, he was about to make him an offer.

In a certain wood of his kingdom there dwelt two giants who did much harm by the way they robbed, murdered, burned, and plundered everything about them; no one could approach them without endangering his life. But if he could overcome and kill these two giants he should have the King's only daughter for a wife, and half his kingdom in the bargain; he might have a hundred horsemen, too, to back him up.

"That's the very thing for a man like me," thought the little tailor, "one doesn't get the offer of a beautiful Princess and half a kingdom every day."

"Done," he answered; "I'll soon put an end to the giants. But I haven't the smallest need of your hundred horsemen; a fellow who can slay seven men at one blow need not be afraid of two."

The little tailor set out and the hundred horsemen followed him. When he came to the outskirts of the wood he said to his followers: "You wait here, I'll manage the giants by myself." He went into the wood, casting his sharp little eyes right and left about him. After a while he spied the two giants lying asleep under a tree and snoring till the very boughs bent with the breeze.

The little tailor lost no time in filling his pack with stones, and then climbed up the tree under which they lay. When he got to the middle of it, he slipped along a branch till he sat just above the sleepers, when he threw down one stone after the other on the nearest giant.

The giant felt nothing for a long time, but at last he woke up, and pinching his companion said, "What did you strike me for?"

"I didn't strike you," said the other, "you must be dreaming."

They both lay down to sleep again, and the tailor threw down a stone on the second giant, who sprang up and cried: "What's that for? Why did you throw something at me?"

"I didn't throw anything," growled the first one. They wrangled on for a time, till, as both were tired, they made up and fell asleep again.

The little tailor began his game once more, and flung the largest stone he could find in his pack with all his force and hit the first giant on the chest. "This is too much of a good thing!" the giant yelled, and springing up like a madman, he knocked his companion against the tree till he trembled. He gave, however, as good as he got, and they became so enraged

The Largest Stone He Could Find

that they tore up trees and beat each other with them till they both fell at once on the ground.

Then the little tailor jumped down. "It's a mercy," he said, "that they didn't root up the tree on which I was perched, or I should have had to jump like a squirrel on to another, which, nimble though I am, would have been no easy job."

He drew his sword and gave each of the giants a thrust or two on the breast, and then went to the horsemen and said: "The deed is done. I've put an end to the two of them; but I assure you it has been no easy matter, for they even tore up trees in their struggle to defend themselves; but all that's of no use against one who slays seven men at one blow."

"Weren't you wounded?" asked the horsemen.

"No fear," answered the tailor. "They haven't touched a hair of my head." But the horsemen wouldn't believe him till they rode into the wood and found the giants and the trees lying around, torn up by the roots.

The little tailor now demanded the promised reward from the King, who

"A Unicorn is Running About Loose"

repented his promise, and pondered once more how he could rid himself of the hero. "Before you obtain the hand of my daughter and half my kingdom," he said, "you must do another deed of valor. A unicorn is running about loose in the wood and doing much mischief. You must first catch it."

"I'm even less afraid of one unicorn than of two giants. Seven at one blow, that's my motto." He took a piece of cord and an ax with him, went out to the wood, and again told the men who had been sent with him to remain outside.

He hadn't to search long, for the unicorn soon passed by, and, perceiving the tailor, dashed straight at him as though it were going to spike him on the spot.

"Gently, gently," said he, "not so fast, my friend," and standing still he waited till the beast was quite near, when he sprang lightly behind a tree.

The unicorn ran with all its force against the tree, and rammed its horn so firmly into the trunk that it had no strength left to pull it out again, and was thus successfully captured.

"Now I've caught my bird," said the tailor,

So the Tailor Became a King

and he came out from behind the tree, placed the cord round its neck, then struck the horn out of the tree with his ax, and, when everything was in order led the beast before the King.

Still the King didn't want to give him the promised reward, and made a third demand. The tailor was to catch a wild boar for him that did a great deal of harm in the wood, and he might have the huntsmen to help him.

"Willingly," said the tailor. "That's mere child's play." But he didn't take the huntsmen into the wood with him, and they were well enough pleased to remain behind, for the wild boar had often received them in a manner which did not make them desire its further acquaintance.

As soon as the boar perceived the tailor it ran at him with foaming mouth and gleaming teeth and tried to knock him down; but our alert little friend ran into a chapel that stood near and got out of the window again with a jump.

The boar pursued him into the church, but the tailor skipped round to the door, and closed it securely. So the raging beast was caught, for it was far too heavy and unwieldly to spring out of the window. The little tailor summoned the huntsmen together, that they might see the prisoner with their own eyes.

Then the hero betook himself to the King, who was obliged now, whether he liked it or not, to keep his promise, and hand over his daughter and half his kingdom. Had he known that no hero-warrior, but only a little tailor, stood before him, it would have gone even more to his heart.

So the wedding was celebrated with much splendor but little joy, and the tailor became a King.

After a time the Queen heard her husband saying one night in his sleep: "My lad, make that waistcoat and patch those trousers, or I'll box your ears." Thus she learned in what rank the young gentleman had been born, and the next day she poured forth her woes to her father, and begged him to help her to get rid of a husband who was nothing more nor less than a tailor.

The King comforted her, and said: "Leave your bedroom door open to-night. My servants shall stand outside, and when your husband is fast asleep they shall enter, bind him fast, and carry him on to a ship, which shall sail away out into the wide ocean."

The Queen was well satisfied with the idea, but the armor-bearer, who had overheard everything, being much attached to his young master, went straight to him and revealed the whole plot.

"I'll soon put a stop to the business," said the tailor. That night he and his wife went to bed at the usual time; when she thought he had fallen asleep she got up, opened the door, and then lay down again.

The little tailor, who had only pretended to be asleep, began to call out in a clear voice: "My lad, make that waistcoat and patch those trousers, or I'll box your ears. I have killed seven at one blow, slain two giants, led a unicorn captive, and caught a wild boar. Why should I be afraid of those men standing outside my door?"

The men, when they heard the tailor saying these words, were so terrified that they fled as if pursued by a wild army, and didn't dare go near him again. So the little tailor was and remained a King all the days of his life!

"The Sky's A-Falling!"

HENNY PENNY

One day Henny Penny was picking up corn in the cornyard

when – whack! – something hit her upon the head. "Goodness gracious me!" said Henny Penny; "the sky's a-going to fall; I must go and tell the King."

So she went along and she went along and she went along till she met Cocky Locky. "Where are you going, Henny Penny?" says Cocky Locky.

"Oh! I'm going to tell the King the sky's a-falling," says Henny Penny.

"May I come with you?" says Cocky Locky.

"Certainly," says Henny Penny. So Henny Penny and Cocky Locky went to tell the King the sky was falling.

They went along, and they went along, and they went along, till they met Ducky Lucky. "Where are you going to, Henny Penny and Cocky Locky?" says Ducky Lucky.

"Oh! we're going to tell the King the sky's a-falling," said Henny Penny and Cocky Locky.

"May I come with you?" says Ducky Lucky.

"Certainly," said Henny Penny and Cocky Locky. So Henny Penny, Cocky Locky, and Ducky Lucky went to tell the King the sky was a-falling.

They went along, and they went along, and they went along, till they met Goosey Loosey. "Where are you going to, Henny Penny, Cocky Locky, and Ducky Lucky?" said Goosey Loosey.

"Oh! we're going to tell the King the sky's a-falling," said Henny Penny and Cocky Locky and Ducky Lucky.

"May I come with you?" said Goosey Loosey.

"Certainly," said Henny Penny, Cocky Locky, and Ducky Lucky. Henny Penny,

Cocky Locky, Ducky Lucky, and Goosey Loosey went to tell the King the sky was a-falling.

So they went along, and they went along, and they went along, till they met Turkey Lurkey. "Where are you going, Henny Penny, Cocky Locky, Ducky Lucky, and Goosey Loosey?" says Turkey Lurkey.

"Oh! we're going to tell the King the sky's a-falling," said Henny Penny, Cocky Locky, Ducky Lucky, and Goosey Loosey.

"May I come with you, Henny Penny, Cocky Locky, Ducky Lucky, and Goosey Loosey?" said Turkey Lurkey.

"Oh, certainly, Turkey Lurkey," said Henny Penny, Cocky Locky, Ducky Lucky, and Goosey Loosey. So Henny Penny, Cocky Locky, Ducky Lucky, Goosey Loosey, and Turkey Lurkey all went to tell the King the sky was a-falling.

They went along, and they went along, and they went along, till they met Foxy Woxy, and Foxy Woxy said to Henny Penny, Cocky Locky, Ducky Lucky, Goosey Loosey, and Turkey Lurkey, "Where are you going Henny

She Never Told the King

Penny, Cocky Locky, Ducky Lucky, Goosey Loosey, and Turkey Lurkey?"

And Henny Penny, Cocky Locky, Ducky Lucky, Goosey Loosey, and Turkey Lurkey said to Foxy Woxy, "We're going to tell the King the sky's a-falling."

"Oh! but this is not the way to the King, Henny Penny, Cocky Locky, Ducky Lucky, Goosey Loosey, and Turkey Lurkey," said Foxy Woxy; "I know the proper way; shall I show it to you?"

"Oh, certainly, Foxy Woxy," said Henny Penny, Cocky Locky, Ducky Lucky, Goosey Loosey, and Turkey Lurkey.

So Henny Penny, Cocky Locky, Ducky Lucky, Goosey Loosey, Turkey Lurkey, and Foxy Woxy all went to tell the King the sky was a-falling.

So they went along, and they went along, and they went along, till they came to a narrow and dark hole. Now this was the door of Foxy Woxy's cave.

But Foxy Woxy said to Henny Penny, Cocky Locky, Ducky Lucky, Goosey Loosey, and Turkey Lurkey, "This is the short way to the King's palace; you'll soon get there if you follow me. I will go first and you come after, Henny Penny, Cocky Locky, Ducky Lucky, Goosey Loosey, and Turkey Lurkey,"

"Why, of course, certainly, without a doubt, why not?" said Henny Penny, Cocky Locky, Ducky Lucky, Goosey Loosey, and Turkey Lurkey.

So Foxy Woxy went into his cave, and he didn't go very far, but turned round to wait for Henny Penny, Cocky Locky, Ducky Lucky, Goosey Loosey, and Turkey Lurkey. So at last, Turkey Lurkey went through the dark hole into the cave. He hadn't got far when "Hrumph," Foxy Woxy snapped off Turkey Lurkey's head and threw his body over his left shoulder.

Then Goosey Loosey went in, and "Hrumph," off went her head and Goosey Loosey was thrown beside Turkey Lurkey.

Then Ducky Lucky waddled down, and "Hrumph," snapped Foxy Woxy, and Ducky Lucky's head was off and Ducky Lucky was thrown alongside Turkey Lurkey and Goosey Loosey.

Then Cocky Locky strutted down into the cave, and he hadn't got far when "Snap! Hrumph!" went Foxy Woxy, and Cocky Locky was thrown alongside of Turkey Lurkey, Goosey Loosey, and Ducky Lucky.

But Foxy Woxy had made two bites at Cocky Locky, and when the first snap only hurt Cocky Locky, but didn't kill him, he called out to Henny Penny. But she turned tail and off she ran home, so she never told the King the sky was a-falling.

TITLES AVAILABLE IN THIS SERIES